Interrupted Bridal Journey
2 books in 1
By: Kent HamiIlton

Copyright ©2019 By: Kelly Curtiss
All rights reserved. No part of this book may be used or reproduced in any matter whatsoever without permission in writing from the author except in the case of brief Quotations embodied in critical articles or review

Part One

By: Kent HamiIlton

Table of Contents
- [Chapter 1](#)
- [Chapter 2](#)
- [Chapter 3](#)
- [Chapter 4](#)
- [Chapter 5](#)
- [Chapter 6](#)

[Chapter 7](#)
- [Chapter 8](#)
- [Chapter 9](#)

Chapter 1

Maryanne opened the letter carefully, and smoothed it out on the table. She began reading.

Dear Maryanne,

I am most pleased to make your acquaintance. As you will see from the letterhead, my name is Thomas Worthington, and I live in San Francisco.

I am a cloth manufacturer and have my own factory which is doing reasonably well. I am 37 years old, and have never been married. This has been mainly due to my spending my time building up my business.

However, I now find that the business doesn't require my full attention, and the need for a feminine influence in my life is becoming apparent. Plus I am becoming aware of the fact that I shall require an heir.

This was the motivation for my contacting Brides By Mail, who put your name forward as a possible wife for me.

They included a photograph in their letter to me, and you seem to be what I am searching for.

I offer you a secure life, free from financial stresses, a large house to run, with servants for the menial chores, and the prospect of having children after an appropriate interval.

Should you accept my offer, kindly reply to this letter. I shall then arrange to wire funds to you for your journey to San Francisco, and other sundries as may be necessary to affect your move. You will be accommodated in a separate part of my house while wedding arrangements are being made, and once married we shall share the main quarters.

I await your reply.

I am, Yours Truly, Thomas Worthington, Esq.

Maryanne sat and looked at the letter. "He does sound a bit stuffy, don't you think, Mr. Tibbles?" She tickled the cat, who replied with an assenting purr. "But a life of relative ease; that's not to be dismissed lightly! Let's ask Aunt Hilda what she thinks."

Maryanne's parents had died while she was young, and she had been raised by her aunt. She, however, had rather narrow views on Maryanne's socializing with the opposite sex, resulting in Maryanne's reaching the age of 23 without any suitors even knowing about her, let alone asking for her hand. For this reason she had decided to contact Brides By Mail. Her aunt had been initially against the idea, but she eventually saw that trying to stop the girl from having a normal life was simply being selfish on her own part, and she had finally assented to the idea.

"Aunt, I have received an offer from a gentleman in San Francisco. Tell me what you think." She gave her aunt the letter.

Aunt Hilda finished reading the letter. She put it down, and then looked at Maryanne. "As much as I shall miss having you around, I do feel it is the best for you. It would seem that he will provide for you handsomely."

"Yes, aunt, but what about love? What about passion? This letter is as dry as dust. And he doesn't even include a photograph of himself! What if I don't like the way he looks?"

"Child, love and passion flare up for a short time, and then you are left with the day to day business of life together. It would be nice to begin with love and passion, but if that doesn't happen, that is a small price to pay for a secure life. Your parents started out with so much love and passion that I was almost jealous of your mother. But it didn't last; it never does. And once they were simply left with each other, and no money to speak of, life became hard. They fought about money almost constantly. Their initial love and devotion didn't stop that. And it was a combination of their penniless state, and their constant warring that contributed to their early deaths. Compare their lives with mine. Your uncle, may he rest in peace, and I never had a day of passion in our lives together, but we had security, and without the constant worry of money, we built up respect and acceptance for each other."

"Respect and acceptance! That sounds so dull! Did you not have any male friends before you met uncle?"

Her aunt looked at her sharply. "I may have, but that is not under discussion right now. I would advise you to consider this offer favorably. Another one like it may not come along for a long time, if at all."

"What do you think, Mr. Tibbles?" enquired Maryanne of the cat. Mr. Tibbles looked at her with his usual non-comprehending look. While thinking "As long as my food bowl is filled every morning, I really don't care what you do!"

Maryanne went and sat on the window seat, and looked out at the gray day. There was a lot of sense in what her aunt said, but at the same time she wished for something more. She had just finished reading Far From the Madding Crowd, and she could not but see Thomas Worthington in the character of Farmer Boldwood. While not exactly putting herself into the role of Bathsheba, she certainly saw the attraction of someone like Sergeant Troy. Someone who was interesting, impulsive, even a little dangerous, but who brought passion to life.

She thought longingly "Can't I just have a little love and passion before settling down?"

Chapter 2

Maryanne slept on the offer, and pondered upon it. Her aunt had brought her up to be sensible and thoughtful, and after a few days she decided that it would be the sensible thing to accept.

She sat down to write to her future husband.

Dear Mr. Worthington...

Too formal. She scrunched the paper up and threw it away.

Dear Thomas...

No, that was too forward. She had not even met him yet! She threw that one away too.

Dear Mr. Worthington,

Thank you for your kind offer of marriage.

I have considered it carefully, and have decided to accept.

I look forward to meeting you, and eventually making you a good wife.

Yours etc.

She thought that if she wrote in the same rather formal and passionless way that his letter had been written, it would please him and smooth their path together. It would not have been appropriate to ask for love and passion when it was reasonably obvious that there was none to be had.

She included details that he would need for the money transfer, sealed it all in an envelope, and placed it on her bedside table.

That night she dreamed that she was now married to Mr. Worthington (she even called him that in her dream). And he DID look exactly like she had imagined Mr. Boldwood to look! They lived in a huge mansion, and there were servants scurrying to and fro everywhere. She could not do anything without a servant jumping to do it for her. It quickly became impossible. If she wanted to write a letter to someone, a servant would whisk the pen and paper away from her and begin writing. If she wanted to read a book, a servant would gently remove the book from her hand and begin reading to her. It became ridiculous. A servant saw her sitting at the window, looking out at the garden, and told her that he would rather look out the window for her, to save her the trouble!

At that point she woke up and lay there wondering about the dream. Could having servants doing all the menial work become irksome? Her aunt had a maid who did cooking and cleaning, but many of the other chores were shared between her and her aunt. She didn't find them to be a bother, and she actually derived some pleasure from doing them well. If she had nothing to do, would she be able to be satisfied with a life of leisure? She came to no definite conclusion.

She posted the letter the next day, and carried on her life as before. A few weeks later a reply arrived from Thomas Worthington.

My Dear Maryanne,

Your reply has filled my heart with gladness!

I am sure you will be very happy here. Every desire of yours, within reason, will be accommodated, and you will have comforts aplenty.

I have arranged to wire sufficient funds to cover your train journey from Baltimore to San Francisco, plus extra for any new clothes that you may require for the journey, and other incidentals.

Kindly contact the Pacific Railroad Company to book your ticket, and inform me of the date of your arrival.

In the meantime I shall instruct the servants to perform a full house cleaning, and specifically the rooms that you will occupy before the wedding.

I reiterate my happiness at your acceptance!

Yours etc.

At least he showed an ability to experience happiness, Maryanne thought; he's not totally devoid of emotion. But still no mention of love or passion. She supposed it was maybe not fair to require love and passion, when Thomas (she made a mental effort to start thinking of him by his first name) had not even met her yet in the flesh, but it would have been pleasant to have a bit more fire in his letter.

The next day she went to the Western Union office to get the money Thomas had wired. She was amazed to discover that he had sent her $300! Way more than was required for a ticket and incidentals.

She then went to the train station, and enquired about trains to San Francisco.

"We have a five day cross-country Pullman service, that leaves every Friday." the clerk told her. "You can have your own compartment, or you can share with other women. Your own costs more. There is a dining car, and the ticket includes three meals a day."

Maryanne decided that with the amount that Thomas had sent her, she could easily afford to have a compartment to herself. Not only did she not have any male friends, but she did not even really have any female friends of her own, and she was not used to spending time in the company of other people, other than her aunt. She had had quite a sheltered upbringing.

Finally the day arrived that she was to leave. She packed the last few things in her trunk, and the two men who were to cart it and them to the station fetched it and placed it in their wagon.

She and Aunt Hilda got into the wagon for the short trip to the station.

"I hope that you are very happy with Mr. Worthington. Let me see, how does it sound: 'Maryanne Worthington'! Very respectable! I am sure that, as long as you look at the entirety of life with him, you will be very happy. He may not sweep you off your feet, but that is overrated anyway!"

"Thanks, aunt. Yes, 'Maryanne Worthington' sounds fine to me too! Don't worry, I shall do my best to make this marriage work. And since it seems I shall be well-to-do, I shall be able to come and see you every so often. Will you be OK without me?"

"Yes, child, I shall be fine. The house will be quieter, no doubt, but Mr. Tibbles and I shall look after each other quite all right."

Maryanne noticed a small tear on her aunt's cheek, and she suddenly hugged her. They had not had a very demonstrative relationship ever, but now, as they were about to part for who knew how long, they hugged each other close.

They parted, and Aunt Hilda blew her nose. "I'm just being silly! I'll see you again soon! Don't worry about me!"

The men carried the trunk through to the platform, and took it to the baggage car. Maryanne and her aunt said their final goodbyes, and Maryanne went to climb aboard. As she did so, she noticed that there were a number of soldiers further down the platform, also busy embarking. She wondered idly why they were there.

Chapter 3

The train pulled out of Baltimore and slowly picked up speed. Maryanne watched the city going by, and gradually thinning out as they left it behind.

Oh well, she thought, phase one of my life is over! I wonder what phase two will bring.

She settled into her compartment. It had almost everything that she needed in what was a very small room. There were two bunks facing each other, one of which converted into a bed. A small table that could fold up out of the way was between them.

She spent the rest of the afternoon reading and updating her diary. It was not always easy to write, what with the constant movement of the train.

Finally, at 6pm, the time they had told her dinner would be served in the dining car, she left her compartment and made her swaying way along the train. At times, as it lurched particularly badly, she used the side of the corridor for support. She wondered if this was what it was like to be drunk.

She reached the dining car, and the maître d' asked her whether she would be prepared to share a table with another couple. She agreed gladly - she was already feeling a little lonely.

The maître d' checked with a middle-aged couple at a table further down the car, who seemed to assent, and he came back and led her to the table. The man stood up, as well as he was able, and bowed to her. "Good evening madam! You are more than welcome to share our table. I am George, and this is my wife Martha. We are the Thackerays."

"Thank you very much. My name is Maryanne Marston." She sat down.

After a minute or two, during which she made her selections from the menu, George addressed her. "So, what is a young woman like you doing crossing this great land of ours alone?" he enquired.

Maryanne saw no reason to be coy about the reason for her journey. "I am on my way to meet my future husband. I am what is known as a mail-order bride."

George's eyebrows shot up, and Martha's eyes opened wide. They were not quite sure what to make of this information.

"Indeed!" exclaimed George. "I had heard of these arrangements, but I have never actually met someone who was undertaking them. May I enquire - please refrain from answering if you would rather not - why you embarked upon this rather unusual method of finding a husband? You are, if I may say so," and here he looked rather nervously at his wife, "quite attractive, and you are obviously educated, so I would have thought that finding a suitable suitor would not have been that difficult."

Maryanne saw no reason not to carry on with her candid admissions. "I was orphaned quite young, and my aunt raised me. Whether she was trying to protect me, in an area in which she felt my parents had failed, or whether she simply didn't see the need for my having an active social life, I'm not quite sure. But I grew up with a very limited circle of acquaintances, amongst which were no suitable men. However, I decided that the life of a spinster did not have great attractions, and so the only other avenue available, that I could see, was this one."

George and Martha digested this information carefully.

Martha spoke. "I think that's a wonderful thing! For a woman to take charge of her life and plot its course on her own - good for you! Too many women these days take whatever life dishes up to them, without striking out in their own direction. I take my hat off to you! Who knows, if I hadn't met George, I might have done the same as you. If these services had existed then. Who is the lucky young man?"

"He's a little bit older than me" said Maryanne. "He's a manufacturer in San Francisco."

"Really!" said George. "May we know his name?"

"Thomas Worthington."

"Bless my soul! We know him well! Who would have guessed!" They all pondered the coincidence that had presented itself. "I may say, without giving too much away, that you are headed for a comfortable life. Thomas's business has done very well, and he will be able to keep you in a way to which I am sure you will easily become accustomed."

"Tell me a bit about him!" asked Maryanne. "His letters were quite formal, and he didn't go into any detail about himself at all."

Martha resumed. "He is a hard worker, and a good man all round. Salt of the earth. I'm sure you'll like him."

Maryanne was painfully aware that Martha made no mention of anything passionate about his nature. He sounded very stolid. And Martha had said 'like', not 'love'.

She was tempted to ask them what it was that had made Thomas decide on a mail-order bride, but thought better of it. It wasn't really their place to surmise on Thomas's reasons, and even if they knew them, it might have been considered disloyal to their friend to mention them to her, who was, at this point anyway, still a stranger to them all.

Maryanne and the couple chatted amiably through the rest of their meal, and they told her what life was like in San Francisco. At least the life there sounded like it was more interesting than where she had come from. Hopefully the environment in which she lived would provide her with some sort of dissipation, even if her home life promised to be rather plain.

After dessert she thanked them for their hospitality and excused herself, and walked back down the dining car on her way to her compartment.

The soldiers that she had noted on the station when she was leaving Baltimore, were sitting at the tables she was passing, and she couldn't help noticing that more than one of them surreptitiously threw an admiring glance at her. She had not been in that many situations where men would admire her, and she found it not altogether unpleasant.

Chapter 4

Maryanne found it surprisingly easy to sleep on the train. The rocking motion was rhythmic, and was not unlike a mother rocking her baby. And although the train was not quiet, the noise was constant and also rhythmic, so after a while one was not even aware of it. She awoke refreshed.

At breakfast George and Martha, and the soldiers, were nowhere to be seen. She ate alone.

She watched the countryside going by. They were in a very deserted area; she assumed it was some part of Indiana. She had perused the route that the train would be taking, when she bought her ticket.

After breakfast she returned to her compartment, and settled in to read her book. After a short while, the train lurched to what seemed to her, a rather sudden stop. She wondered what the cause was.

She opened the window and put her head out to see. A second later, there was a loud crack, and the wood above her head splintered. At the same time, the compartment door was flung open and one of the soldiers, holding a rifle, rushed into the compartment and pulled her in from the window. "Get down on the floor!" he shouted at her. He then looked carefully out the window, before loosing off a couple of shots himself. Maryanne had never heard anything as loud as the noise of the rifle. Her ears were ringing. At that, the train started up again, and picked up speed quite quickly. The soldier kept a vigil at the window for another minute or two, before turning to look at Maryanne.

"You can get up now!" he smiled. "Sorry about that! I didn't have time for explanations! If you'd stayed there, who knows, their next shot might have found its target!"

"Thank you! Who was that, that was shooting at the train?" Maryanne resumed her seat.

The soldier, without any invitation, sat down on the bunk opposite her. "Shawnees. There are still small pockets of them resisting white settlement. They put a rock on the line to make the train stop, and then they were going to ambush it. But they hadn't bargained on getting the reception that they did! We were waiting for them. This stretch has this sort of thing happen occasionally, and that's why we are here, to protect you fine folk!"

"I wondered why there were soldiers on the train."

"I heard the shot, just as I was passing your compartment, and I saw that they were shooting at you. So I decided that the last thing I wanted was to have a bullet mar that pretty face!"

Maryanne blushed slightly.

"We saw you at dinner last night. Was that your parents you were sitting with?"

"No, I met those people only then myself! I am travelling alone."

"Really! Leaving your husband, or returning to your husband? Whoops, sorry, I am forgetting my manners." He stood up. "I am Peter Simpson. How do you do?" He bowed, and extended his hand to take hers.

"How do you do? I am Maryanne Marston." Peter kissed her hand lightly, and reseated himself.

Maryanne found his rather forward questioning a little unusual, but she was not used to dissembling to people, so she answered plainly. "Neither, actually. Well, he's not my husband yet, anyway. I am travelling to meet my future husband. I am a mail-order bride."

Peter bent forward and looked at her keenly. "Why, in all the world, would someone as pretty as you need to be a mail-order bride?"

Maryanne gave the same basic explanation that she had to the couple at dinner the previous evening.

"You mean there were no real males, in your vicinity that had the gumption to ask for your hand! I had always wondered about the so-called men of Baltimore. They are living up to their reputation! If I had been around, that situation would have been different! Mail-order bride! This is a travesty!"

Maryanne wasn't sure whether she should be upset at what Peter was saying. But she supposed that he was casting aspersions more on the men of her home town, than on her. She decided to give him the benefit.

"And who is this lucky man that is waiting for you at the end of the line?"

"Thomas Worthington. He is a successful business owner."

"Never heard of him. Why does HE need to order a bride by mail order? Why can't he find a woman locally?" Maryanne bridled a little at that, and Peter checked himself. "Sorry, that is not really my business. I withdraw the question!" he said with a smile.

"Well, if you really want to know, he has been building his business for the last few years, and has not been able to take time out to seek a wife." Maryanne found herself almost needing to apologize for Thomas.

"Hmm. Those sorts of men might become married, but their business remains their mistress! After not having time for a woman for so many years, I hope he manages to find the time for you!"

Maryanne shrugged. "Possibly not as much as I should like, but the ease of life will compensate for that. He seems to be very well-off."

"You think that money can make up for love? I'm afraid I can't agree! Love is all that is worth fighting for. Money simply keeps you warm at night."

Maryanne replied "I have no experience of either, so I'll take what you say under advisement."

Peter stood up. He looked down at her. "I call it criminal that a woman like you might never know real love, real passion! Au revoir!" and he left.

Maryanne sat there, thinking about what he had said. His final remark echoed through her head, and gnawed at her resolve.

Chapter 5

When it came time for lunch, Maryanne wended her way to the dining car as before. As she entered, she saw George and Martha at their table, and she began walking to it. However, she almost immediately found her way blocked by Peter Simpson.

"My dear Miss Marston, would you be so good as to grace our table with your presence?" She could not decide whether he was teasing her or not, with his exaggerated speech. There were two other soldiers at the table with him, who both stood up.

"Please, we would be honored," the one said.

"It would make our day!" said the other.

The Thackerays hadn't actually noticed her arrival yet, and so she decided that there could be no harm. She sat down. The rest of them sat down. The other two soldiers were introduced by Peter as Stephen and Andrew.

Maryanne addressed the other two. "So, who did you two rescue this morning, while Peter here was holding the entire Shawnee nation at bay on my behalf?" She had decided that, if Peter was going to exaggerate, she could match him.

"Oh, no such derring-do on our part, I'm afraid," Stephen said. "We just gave cover to the engineer who had to go and remove the rocks from the line. Saw one or two of them in the distance, but they were no real threat. But I believe Peter had to pull you in from the window! He's so rough!" he said with a grin.

"Yes, I know," said Maryanne. "I still have the bruises!"

Peter laughed. "I did apologize afterwards, remember! Rather a bruise than a bullet, don't you think?"

"Yes, indeed," said Maryanne.

The four of them made polite conversation for a few minutes more, and then Stephen and Andrew got up to leave. "Please excuse us." Stephen said. "We had already eaten when you arrived, and we need to attend to some things." They went and left Peter and Maryanne alone.

"So you're going all the way through to San Francisco," mused Peter. "We'll be leaving the train at Omaha."

"Oh, why is that?" asked Maryanne.

"We are based in Omaha. We leave the train, and another platoon takes over from Omaha to the coast. We go back to our barracks, and then get on the train again on its way back East."

"I see. And what do you do in your barracks while waiting for the train to return?"

"Play cards. Polish our boots. Clean our kit. Occasionally we are required to go on patrols in areas where the Indians are up to something, but generally we have a lot of time to spare. But enough about me. I want to find out more about you."

"I am not very interesting, I am afraid."

"Oh, I am sure you are. You just don't know all the things about you that I shall find interesting! Where were you born?"

"In Baltimore."

"You said earlier that you were orphaned, and that you had a rather secluded upbringing with your aunt."

"Oh, so you remember what I told you!"

"Oh yes, I remember everything you told me! But did you not have ANY men friends? To take you to balls, the opera, concerts, that sort of thing?"

"No, nothing like that. Occasionally my aunt and I would go to a concert, or the opera, but I never went with a man."

"Hm. I can't help feeling that you need to see a little more of life before you settle down with the worthy Mr. Worthington."

"Oh you do, do you? You know about these things?"

"Indeed I do. And I happen to know exactly the right man to do it!"

Maryanne was not so inexperienced as to misunderstand his offer. She just looked at him and smiled.

"Come, finish your dessert, and then I want to show you something," Peter said.

Chapter 6

She finished eating, and they got up. By now George and Martha had noticed her. She waved at them, and they waved back. They watched her and Peter departing together, for a little longer than was required.

Peter led her into the next car, and along the length of its corridor. As they reached the coupling between that car and the following one, he stopped. They were standing between the cars, with the countryside rushing past on either side.

"Right, follow me," he said. He began climbing up the ladder on the end of the one car. Maryanne looked slightly alarmed. But she followed him anyway. He reached the top, and heaved himself onto the top of the car. She climbed up until her head was higher than the roof of the car. The wind rushing past tousled her hair.

"I can't get on top there, it's too high!" she shouted, to be heard above the wind.

"I'll help you!" he shouted back.

Peter found purchase with his foot on a jutting out part of the roof, and then part helped, and part pulled Maryanne on to the top of the car. She knelt facing the direction they were moving, with the wind blowing her hair around her face. Then she turned to sit next to him.

They sat there, watching the smoke rise from the engine at the front, the grass and trees rushing past on either side, all the way to the distant mountains. She had never felt so alive in her life. She whooped with joy. "I've never done anything like this before!" she shouted at Peter. For some reason that she could not fathom, she was not afraid.

"We're just getting started!" he replied.

After a minute or two of sitting like this, the train went around a gentle curve, and up ahead they suddenly saw a tunnel. "What do we do now?" she shouted.

"You lie face down. And keep your eyes and mouth shut!"

"Why?"

"You'll see!"

Peter crawled a short distance away from her, and then lay face down on the roof, facing the front. She did the same, where she was, and raised her head to watch the tunnel get closer and closer. As the engine went into the tunnel, she suddenly understood the reason for Peter's advice. Without the open air around it, the smoke from the engine was now confined inside the tunnel. As they went into the tunnel she dropped her head and closed her mouth and eyes tight. The noise, which had been considerable before, now became deafening, as the sound of the engine, the wind and the noise of the car itself, all reverberated inside the tunnel. But what was most amazing to her was smoke from the engine. It was both hot, and full of little particles of soot. As she lay there the hot smoke and the soot swirled around her, and she could feel the soot touching her skin and even getting into her ears. It was a sensory excess.

Finally she heard the sound from the engine diminish, and she realized that it was back in the open. She kept her head down, and a few seconds later she saw sunlight again behind her eyelids, and opened her eyes. Raising her head, she could not stop laughing. "That was amazing! I think I've got soot everywhere!" she shouted at Peter.

He returned to where she was. "You have it in your hair, and all over your face!" he laughed.

"So do you!" she returned. The strange thing about the soot was that it didn't smudge and leave streaks on her skin. The particles were hard, and could be brushed off quite easily. After another minute or two in the wind, most of the soot in her hair and on her face had been blown off.

"Have you had enough?" he asked.

"Yes, OK."

She crawled backwards to the ladder, and with his help managed to work her way over the edge and get her footing on it again. She climbed back down, shortly followed by Peter. They stood there laughing.

"That was the strangest thing I've done in my life!" she said. "I suppose you do it every trip!"

"No, actually, not. I have been on top of the car before, but it's the first time I've been through a tunnel."

"So how did you know it was safe! What if the gap between the car and the roof of the tunnel had been too small, and we had been swept off the car?"

"I didn't know. There was not enough time to get down from the roof when we saw the tunnel, so I took a chance. Carpe Diem! But I knew about the smoke from times I've been into a tunnel with the compartment window open." He looked at the side of her head. "You have a whole tender of coal in your ears! You'd better go and wash. But please don't do anything with your hair! The wind has teased it into a magnificent frame for your face!"

"I don't believe you! It's you who's teasing me!" She felt her hair with her hand, and it seemed to have twice the volume it usually had.

"OK, you go back to your compartment, and sort yourself out. I'll be along in half an hour to show you something else."

And so they parted, with Maryanne wondering what Peter planned to show her next.

Chapter 7

She returned to her compartment, and washed her face and ears, brushed her hair, and changed her dress. The one she had been wearing was scuffed with dirt from crawling around on the roof. She then tried to read, but could not concentrate on her book, so she sat watching the trees rush past.

Promptly after half an hour, there was a knock on her door. Peter stood there, with his rifle. He came into the compartment, and sat down, leaving the door open.

"Have you ever used a firearm?" he asked.

"No" replied Maryanne.

"Would you like to give it a try?"

"Why not? This is not turning out to be a normal day in any other way, so why stop now?"

Peter gave her a quick lesson on the different parts of the rifle, and how to hold it, with the butt against her shoulder, and to look along the sights. He helped her get it into position by putting his arms around her shoulders and supporting its weight while she settled herself under it. She was acutely aware of his proximity; she had never been so close to a man before. He released his hold on the rifle and allowed her to take its full weight.

He opened the window. "OK, fire away when you're ready. Just keep the butt pressed hard into your shoulder!"

She squinted down the sights, and aimed at a tree passing in the distance, and squeezed the trigger. She knew that it was going to be loud, from Peter's firing it during the ambush, but with her ear that much closer to it now, the noise was incredible. Plus, the kick back into her shoulder was violent.

She lowered the rifle, and handed it back to Peter. "Thanks, once is enough! How does your shoulder take all that punishment?" she said, massaging her shoulder ruefully.

"You get used to it." He removed the magazine and made the rifle safe, and then propped it against the wall of the compartment.

He rummaged in his pocket and brought out a pack of cards. He shuffled them, and then fanned them out towards her. "Take any card, look at it without showing me, and then replace it anywhere you like."

She did as instructed. He shuffled the cards again, and then fanned them towards himself. He removed one, and showed it to her. "This was your card."

Her eyes widened. "How did you do that?"

"A magician never divulges his secrets! You'd have to torture me."

"That could be arranged!"

He smiled. "If I were going to be tortured, I cannot imagine anyone I would rather have torture me than you!"

Maryanne blushed.

Maryanne and Peter spent the rest of the afternoon together. He told her stories of his exploits as a soldier, and she listened with growing enchantment. He pointed out interesting landmarks that they were passing, and related incidents that had happened there, where he knew the details. He had a smattering of botanical knowledge too, and he showed her some of the trees and flowers that he knew. They saw a herd of bison at one stage, and they watched them and marveled at their size and powerful build.

Maryanne found him to be interesting and stimulating. She had never known that the company of someone else could be such fun. He left her late in the afternoon, and she decided not to eat in the dining car this evening, but to take a small meal in her compartment. Within a short time of his leaving her, she found that she was missing his company. She wondered whether this was normal so soon after meeting a person.

She tried to read, but after re-reading the same sentence five times, without comprehending anything, she gave up and watched the sunset. Her mind was in a whirl.

Chapter 8

That night Maryanne did not sleep well. She wondered whether it was the rocking of the train, but that had not prevented her from sleeping well the first night. She knew that she was severely troubled.

In the short time she had known Peter Simpson, she had realized that a man could be fun to be with, could be interesting and stimulating. Peter was all these things, and when she compared him with the sort of man that Thomas Worthington had projected himself to be, via his letters, she found Peter by far the more attractive person.

She decided to try and winkle more information out of the Thackerays. She went to breakfast, and luckily they were there, and Peter was not. She asked if she might join them again, and they assented gladly.

After giving her order to the steward, and after waiting what seemed an appropriate interval so as not to make it seem that it was the primary purpose of her visit, she asked "Tell me a little more about Thomas. What sort of person is he? Is he fun to be with?"

Martha immediately knew where Maryanne was coming from. Her feminine instinct understood exactly what was going on. George, as with most males, was blissfully unaware of Maryanne's real reason, and took her question at face value. He replied, "Fun to be with is a bit strong to describe him. He's pleasant, and he knows a lot about cloth." Maryanne nodded.

Martha was faced with a dilemma. Should she sell Thomas hard, and paint a glamorous picture of him for Maryanne? Or should she tell it like it is, that Thomas was decidedly not fun to be with, but was a good man nonetheless. She tried to steer a middle path. "Thomas is interesting in his own way, and once you get to know that way, you will find him good company."

Maryanne, however, for all her naïveté, could see right through what Martha was saying. She had her fair share of feminine intuition too. To her, it shouted "Dull, dull, dull!"

They made desultory conversation for the rest of the meal, and Maryanne returned to her compartment to agonize.

She realized that she was not actually sure what she was agonizing about, other than whether to carry on to San Francisco and her fate with Thomas Worthington. Peter had not made any suggestion, or any sort of offer, so it was not as if there was a clear alternative. She was just coming to the inescapable conclusion that she could not carry on with the marriage arrangement with Thomas. With people like Peter in the world, the Thomas's didn't stand a chance.

There was a knock at her door. She opened it, and Peter stood there. "Good morning, Miss Muffett! How did you sleep?"

"Passing well, thank you. And you?"

"Wonderfully! May I come in?"

She retreated into the compartment. Peter came in, and this time closed the door behind him.

He sat on the bunk opposite her, and looked at her. He didn't say anything. She returned his gaze levelly.

He looked out the window, and suddenly seemed to get an idea. He went to it, opened it and looked out. They were at that stage passing through a cutting, where there was bushy vegetation growing up the bank, quite close to the train line. He waited for a few seconds, and then lunged outward. He came away from the window with a flower in his hand. He closed the window, and sat down again. He looked at her.

"Maryanne..."

She waited. She looked at him.

"Maryanne, this may seem totally precipitate, and I suppose it is. Since the moment I set eyes upon you, I have felt this keen attraction. And after spending a large part of the day with you yesterday, I have come to the realization that I don't want to spend a large part of any day in the future, without you. I know you are promised to another man, but I would ask you to reconsider. What I'm saying, Maryanne, is will you marry me?" He slid off the bunk and kneeled before her, offering her the flower, and looking up at her.

She had imagined this moment happening to her, from books she had read, and she had seen an ill-defined suitor, in her imagination, kneeling in front of her. The fact that she and Thomas had discussed marriage, by letter, in a cold and dispassionate way, was yet another reason that she had thought their relationship was doomed. Here was Peter, whose company she adored, and who now professed to adore her company too. There was really no other answer.

"Yes, I shall," she said simply, and took the flower.

Peter stood up, took her hands, and raised her to stand in front of him. "You have made me so happy!" He kissed her tenderly.

Maryanne's first kiss with another man was a defining moment in her life. She felt a thousand emotions all fighting for dominance in her heart. Love, happiness, relief, bliss, plus all shades and combinations of these. There was tumult in her brain.

Finally they sat down on the bunk together, holding hands.

Peter explained. "If our journey on this train had been longer, I would have given you more time to get to know me, before asking you. But as you know, we are due in Omaha tomorrow, and I would never have forgiven myself to let you disappear over the horizon without asking you. I am so glad I did!"

"I am glad you did too!" She placed her head on his shoulder, and experienced an all-encompassing feeling of peace and wellbeing. She was blissfully happy.

She and Peter spent the rest of the morning talking about their future. He went back to his compartment for lunch, and Maryanne remained in hers.

Chapter 9

After lunch, Maryanne decided that she had to tell George and Martha Thackeray about the situation, and request their assistance. She found out from the conductor where their compartment was, and made her way there. She knocked on the door.

Martha opened it. "Oh, hello my dear! How are you this fine afternoon?"

"I am well, thank you. May I have a word with you and George?"

"Certainly! Come in."

Maryanne sat on a bunk, and faced the two of them with trepidation. She took a deep breath.

"I have to tell you something that may shock you. And I also wish you to pass on a message for me." The two of them looked at her impassively. "I don't know whether you have noticed that I have been spending a lot of time with one of the soldiers on the train. He came to my rescue when we were ambushed by the Shawnee, and since then we have developed a relationship. He has shown me a side of life that I never knew existed, and I have to say that I have been swept off my feet!"

There was still no response from George or Martha. They simply listened.

"I have come to the very difficult decision to leave the train at Omaha, with Peter. That is his name. I had read about love at first sight, but I always thought that it was a fiction. However, it has happened to me, and it is very real! Peter has proposed to me, and I have accepted."

At this the older couple showed signs of life. They raised their eyebrows perceptibly.

"You may think it is foolish. I am sure you do. A girl like me, with no experience in the ways of the world, apparently throwing away a secure future for something that has no guarantees at all. You may be totally right. But I cannot deny my heart. If I were to stay with the train all the way to San Francisco, I should always pine for a life that I never had. I should be an unhappy and morose wife, which is not what Thomas deserves. He may not see it this way initially, but I really think that this is for his own good in the long run too. I came to tell you of the situation, since you had been kind to me and shown an interest in me. But in addition I should ask you a favor; that you inform Thomas of what has happened and explain it to him so that he may understand. Would you be able to do that for me?"

Martha took a long sigh. "My dear, I do understand. I have known of affairs of the heart. You are in the unenviable position of having two options, neither of which is ideal. As you say, if you were to carry to Thomas, you would always wonder what life with Peter would have been like. But at the same time, I am reasonably sure that you will find that life as a soldier's wife is far from wonderful too. You will never have enough money to live comfortably, and once the initial bliss has worn off, concern for money is all that will occupy your days. I just wish for your sake that you had had more experience of passion when you were younger. A heady romance or two satisfies the hunger for this sort of thing, gets it out of your system, and prepares you for settling down and embarking on the next loving phase of your life, which is that for your children, and which lasts until the end of your life."

George added "I am afraid that you are making a great mistake, but I can see that there would be no talking you out of it. I wish you whatever luck you can find." George seemed to be somewhat exasperated by Maryanne's decision.

Martha resumed. "We shall inform Thomas as gently as we can. I cannot guarantee that he will take it lightly, and I doubt that he will see that it is in his own interests. But we shall do our best."

Maryanne spoke "I shall also write to him, and set out my feelings as plainly as possible. But since you know him, I felt it would be so much better if you could explain the situation to him. Thank you very much."

Maryanne took her leave of the couple, who seemed now somewhat weighed down by the responsibility that she had placed on them. They did not look forward to having to disappoint Thomas at the station in San Francisco, as he waited there for his bride-to-be.

Chapter 10

The following morning, with a mix of apprehensiveness and happiness, Maryanne made preparations for disembarking from the train at Omaha. Shortly before they arrived there, Peter dropped by.

"Are you absolutely sure you want to do this?" he asked.

"Are YOU sure that you want ME to do this?" she countered.

"I couldn't be more sure of anything in the world." he replied.

"Then I am sure too."

He put his arms around her and they had a long embrace.

"I need to get back to my platoon. I'll see you on the station. I have arranged for your trunk to be removed from the baggage car."

"Thank you."

She sat and watched the passing scene show more and more signs of habitation, as they approached Omaha. Only two days ago she had wondered what this new phase of her life would bring. She could never have anticipated the right angle turn it was about to take.

They arrived in Omaha, and she alighted from the train. Her trunk was brought to her by two men, who asked her what she wanted to do with it. She asked them to take it to the waiting room. As she was following them, she saw George and Martha watching from the window of their compartment. She ran up to them. "Please try and understand! I know you think this is madness. And please try and get Thomas to understand!"

Martha smiled and said she would try. George couldn't manage a smile, even though he knew he should.

Maryanne met Peter outside the station. "OK, where to now?" she chirped happily.

"Just one item of business before we leave. Let's go to the ticket office and cash in the second half of your ticket."

"I didn't know you could do that!"

They went and spoke to the ticketing clerk, and after he had conferred with his manager, they were paid out $80, half the original cost of the ticket.

Peter hired a carriage, and he and the two men loaded her trunk into it. He tipped them generously. He helped Maryanne up into the carriage, and took the reins.

"I know a very comfortable boarding house, that is only 3 blocks from the barracks. That's where you're going to be installed!"

They rode off into the town, found the boarding house, and Peter made the necessary arrangements with the landlady.

"You settle in here, and I'll be back in the morning, and we can start making arrangements for the wedding." He kissed her tenderly, and took his leave.

Maryanne unpacked her clothes, and had a long bath. She found that travelling by train had left her feeling somewhat grubby.

After her bath, she felt that she could put off no longer the two letters that she knew she had to write.

Neither was going to be easy, but she started with the one to Aunt Hilda, since she thought it would not be as difficult.

Dear Aunt Hilda,

I am sure you are wondering why you are getting a letter from me postmarked Omaha. I am afraid that there has been a change in plan. I'm sure you won't like it, but hopefully you will understand when you hear the circumstances.

On the train, I met a soldier from the Omaha barracks. He saved me from getting shot at by some Shawnee who ambushed the train. Since that time, he and I have been in almost constant company, and aunt, I have never felt as happy as I do with him. He is funny, considerate, adventurous (he took me on to the top of the one cars, while the train was going, and we even went through a tunnel!) and he makes me feel alive in a way that I have never felt before. He has proposed to me, and I have accepted. We are now in Omaha (he is still in his barracks, and I am temporarily staying in a boarding house), and very shortly we are to be married.

I can almost hear your exclamations of dismay as you read this. I know it must seem that I am very foolish, impetuous, and have no concern for the future. Those may all be true, but I could not carry on with the train after Omaha, and leave behind a life that, while possibly uncertain, offers adventure and thrill. You know the reservations that I had about Mr. Worthington. Life with him promised to be easy, but so dull!

Please do not think ill of me, aunt. I am sure that, if you had had the same upbringing as me, and were thrust into the same situation, you would have taken the same course of action.

Your loving niece,
Maryanne.

That wasn't too bad, thought Maryanne. Now for the tough one!

Dear Mr. Worthington,

I am sure that by the time you read this, you will have been informed by George and Martha Thackeray of the change of situation.

I am profoundly sorry for any hurt that this might have caused you, and please understand that, if there were any way that I could have done this without affecting you, I would have. However, I could see no such path.

My decision was not taken lightly, and I considered all angles of which I was aware.

The man I am to marry is kind, considerate and loving. He is all that I want. I am sure that a simple girl like me would have proved inadequate to your lifestyle requirements eventually.

I shall arrange to reimburse the $300 you sent me as soon as I am able to.

Yours with apologies,
Maryanne Marston.

She decided that she had better leave out any reference to the fun, adventure and passion for life that she expected with Peter, since it would have implied that she had no such expectations for her life with Thomas. It was the truth, but she didn't want to hurt him any more than she no doubt would shortly be doing. Also, she had promised to pay back the $300, but she had no idea where she would find the money to do so. She resolved to worry about that later.

After a light supper in the boarding house dining room (which, she reflected ruefully, bore no comparison to the luxury of the train dining car), she retired to bed, and dreamt of happy times to come.

Chapter 11

Peter came to the boarding house the next day, and they sat in the parlor. Men were not allowed into the single women's rooms.

"Right, Manny, we have a busy day ahead of us." He had already assigned Maryanne a nickname. She tried to think of a similar one for him, but could not come up with anything. "We need to arrange the preacher for the wedding, and then find a suitable house to rent."

"OK, I'm ready! Let's hit the trail!"

They went to a church that Peter had thought would be suitable, and spoke to the pastor. He agreed to perform the ceremony that Saturday afternoon. Then they started looking for a place to stay. That proved somewhat more difficult, since Peter's salary did not extend to anything other than the cheapest available, and there were not many that were available. However, they eventually found a very small rough clapboard single story house in a side street, that was just affordable, and was currently vacant, thus allowing them to have access immediately, and to move in right after the wedding.

They then had to find something with which to furnish it, and they discovered the difficulties of setting up home where neither had any family nearby who could have lent or contributed any items. They scoured the second hand shops and pawn shops for suitable pieces, with the refund from the train ticket coming in handy. After hiring a cart to move the items to the house, they eventually they had the rudiments of a home set up. They sat in the parlor, in two old chairs that they had bought, and surveyed the house.

"So, Manny my love, what do you think? Is this going to be enough for you? I know it's not quite the same style as Mr. Worthington would have provided, but it will be enough for us to start with, what do you say?"

"Please stop comparing yourself with Mr. Worthington! If I'd wanted to marry him I would have stayed on the train! I am here because I love you, and we are going to make a happy home here!" She got up and went and sat on his lap and hugged him. He returned the hug.

Over the next few days they returned to the house each day, to clean it up, add further smaller items of furniture, and generally make it into a friendly abode. Peter cleared some weeds from the garden and threw out some old rusty items that lay around. Maryanne managed to find some cheap material in a local haberdasher, and with it she sewed some curtains for the bedroom and the parlor. As each worked away, he or she would occasionally stop and look at the other, and feel that life was good. In the evening, in the boarding house, Maryanne added some frills to an existing white dress of hers, to make a passable wedding outfit. They waited impatiently for their wedding day.

Finally the day of the wedding arrived. Peter, with Stephen as his best man, arrived at the church in his best dress uniform, well in time. Maryanne had made friends with her landlady's daughter, and had asked her if she would be her bridesmaid. She jumped at the opportunity. They arrived at the church a little after the specified time, as is a bride's privilege. Without a father or any other male relative to give her away, Maryanne walked down the aisle alone. A few strangers had come to the church to pray, and they stayed and watched.

The ceremony went off without incident, and they finally walked back down the aisle as man and wife. The four of them went to celebrate at a local tea house, and had their fill of tea, coffee and fresh cream cakes. Stephen and the landlady's daughter seemed to get along admirably, and Peter winked at Maryanne when Stephen asked her if she would accompany him to an upcoming regimental dance.

After the tea, the happy couple walked to their new house. Peter carried Maryanne over the threshold, and then placed her gently down in the parlor. "So, what's it like to be Mrs. Simpson?" he asked.

"Mr. and Mrs. Simpson. It sounds wonderful!" They hugged each other.

Let us draw a curtain on our view of their lives at this point.

Chapter 12

Maryanne and Peter settled into married life in their little clapboard dwelling. Maryanne knew, from his initial description of his life as a soldier, that he would be away roughly half the time, on the train as it went from Omaha to Baltimore and back again, and she could accept this, since for the other half of the time, she had him to herself, apart from his occasional duties at the barracks. As a married man, he was relieved of some of these.

During the times he was away she busied herself with making the house into a home. She sewed, cleaned, and even learned how to paint the rather dull furniture which was all that they had been able to afford. She had learned the basics of cooking and baking from her aunt, but she now threw herself into becoming accomplished in this area.

During the times they were together they talked, laughed, went for walks, and reveled in each other's company. He showed her around his barracks, and she met Stephen again, who informed her that he and her ex-landlady's daughter were now walking out together. This made her glad; that the culmination of her and Peter's happiness had contributed to the happiness of two other people.

Maryanne felt that life could not make her happier. Until the day she awoke feeling a little odd. She had never felt this way before, and she had no idea what it could be. It was not that she was unwell, but something certainly was different. She put it down to something she might have eaten.

When the following day, and the next, it had not gone away, but had in fact increased slightly, she became a little worried. She went to see the doctor. He told her what her Aunt Hilda ought to have explained.

She got home, and it was luckily a time when Peter was home, since she didn't know how she would have kept the news bottled up for days if he had not been there.

She found him in the garden, planting some radishes. "Peter, love, you soon will have someone to help you in the garden!"

He stood up, and looked mystified for a second. But when he saw her unconsciously move her hand across her stomach, he understood. He dropped his trowel and enveloped her in a huge hug. "That's wonderful! I can't wait!"

They stood there in each other's arms. Maryanne thought back to her life just three short months ago, and how it had changed. She had found the man of her dreams, who had made her very happy. And now that she was to have a baby, her happiness was complete.

Maryanne resumes her journey
Interrupted Bridal Journey
Part two
By: Kent Hamillton

Table of Contents
- Chapter 1
- Chapter 2
- Chapter 3
- Chapter 4
- Chapter 5
- Chapter 6
- Chapter 7

Chapter 8
- Chapter 9
- Chapter 10

Chapter 1

Maryanne ran her hand for the thousandth time over her stomach. The thought that there was a budding life inside it filled her with wonder. There was still no external evidence of her pregnancy, since she was only two months into her term, but she certainly felt different. Partly physically, and she had occasional morning sickness, but far more emotionally. She felt more in tune with God or The Universe, she wasn't sure which, and that she was fulfilling her destiny in some way. There is little that is more satisfying, and little that leads to a greater feeling of completeness, than the conviction that one is fulfilling one's life's work. Plus she felt it brought her and Peter closer together.

Peter, since he didn't have a new life growing inside of him, couldn't feel the same way as Maryanne. However, he was able to see that her pregnancy was making her blossom, and that made him happy. Their life together was idyllic. Although she missed him while he was away on his duties, the time they spent together when he was back in Omaha, made up for it amply.

At about two months into her pregnancy, a letter arrived postmarked Baltimore. Maryanne left it on the kitchen table for two days before opening it; she dreaded its contents, and the inevitable pall that she assumed it would cast over everything. She finally decided she could delay it no longer.

Dear Child,

Your letter both saddened and gladdened my heart. Talk about trying to confuse an old lady!

I am sure that you expect me to tell you that you have made a mistake, and that you will regret this, and all kinds of similar admonishments. And, yes, these may all be true. You have made a mistake, in the long term, and you may very well regret this. But I understand that, at this time, you are exceedingly happy, and that alone is enough to give me joy.

When we were discussing your marriage to Mr. Worthington, you made reference to my possibly having had male friends before meeting your uncle, and you may have inferred from my reaction that there was more to that subject than I had previously admitted. There is a lot from my younger days that I never told you. There's a lot that I never told your uncle, too! Maybe now is as good a time as any to unburden myself. I have carried the secret for too long.

I did meet a man before your uncle, and we were very much in love. I fell pregnant, and since we were not married, and there was no prospect of that happening, I had to go away for a time. The scandal of an unwed mother in our family would have broken it, if it had become generally known, and so they manufactured a reason for my leaving. I had the baby, and immediately gave it up for adoption. After a suitable interval I returned. The man I was in love with came with me initially, but as I got larger and larger from the pregnancy, his interest waned, and not long before I gave birth he disappeared. I have never seen him, or the child I gave birth to, since.

That is one of the main reasons that, when your parents died within a short time of each other, I was more than happy to take you in. You were the child that I could never have kept. By that time I was married to your uncle, and it seemed that we could not have any children, and we were reasonably financially secure, so it all worked out. And, if I may say so, raising you was one of the most rewarding things I have ever done!

I feel better for having shared that! It's been sitting heavily on my heart for many a year. The fling that I had, although unplanned, got the need for heady romance out of me, and made me content with your uncle. And contentment is more than one can expect out of life!

I hope you don't think any the worse of me after this revelation. I imagine not, since I was subject to the same desires and influences that you were. You at least have put the horse before the cart!

The only advice I can give you is to hold fast to the joy you are currently experiencing, and remember it well. Since there is every likelihood that times will get tougher. Things change, men's attentions change, what was a joy becomes a burden. I don't wish these changes on you; however I anticipate them from experience.

I hope that your joy remains for as long as it may.

Your loving,

Aunt Hilda.

Maryanne sat and looked out the window. She understood that things could change. However, the way she felt now, it seemed that her happiness could go on forever.

A few weeks later, a letter arrived from San Francisco. This was the one Maryanne had been dreading the most. This time, however, since she didn't waste time before reading it; she didn't want the prospect looming over her like a cloud, any longer than necessary.

Dear Maryanne,

I don't need to tell you that your actions have surprised me immensely. Throwing over a comfortable, secure prospect, for what can only be described as uncertainty and almost guaranteed penury, leaves me at a loss for explanation. However, the very limited interaction that I have had with the opposite sex has shown me that many of their actions are without logical cause.

You may care to picture the scene in your mind. My standing on the platform at San Francisco station, flowers in hand, awaiting with interest to see you alight. When instead, George and Martha Thackeray disembark, and come and break the news to me as gently as they are able. It put me in the role of the jilted suitor, one in which I had no experience, and for which I have no particular taste.

I don't mind telling you that, from the time of your acceptance letter, until the news was broken to me by the Thackerays, I built up an image in my mind of us happily married, with you ensconced in my house, and a few children added to the scene after a while. The bombshell delivered by the Thackerays effectively destroyed that image.

However, if you were to see sense now, I would be prepared to forgive, and allow us to return to our previous plan. I could arrange to have your marriage to this soldier annulled, and we could resume where we left off, effectively. I urge you to consider the future, and take me up on this offer.

Yours etc.

Thomas Worthington.

The letter depressed Maryanne rather. She had not wanted to hurt or disappoint Thomas, but it was obvious that she had. The image of his waiting expectantly at the station was rather pathetic, and she was grieved to have been the cause of it.

The possibility of taking up his offer did not cross her mind for a second as a pursuable option, but she wondered whether he would have made the offer had he known of her imminent confinement.

Luckily he had not mentioned the money. It would seem that the money was the least of his concerns. She was glad of that, since she still had no idea how she was going to repay him. Peter's salary was not large, and most of it seemed to be consumed by their living expenses.

She put the letter away and resolved not to answer it. She had made things plain in her most recent letter to Thomas, and there was no point in reiterating her feelings.

Chapter 2

About five months later, during a period when Peter was away on duty, Maryanne was sitting at home, crocheting some baby clothes, when there was a knock at the door. She opened it, to reveal a prosperous looking gentleman on the doorstep. He said nothing. She was about to ask what she could do for him, when she realized who it had to be.

"Hello, Thomas."

"Hello, Maryanne."

They stood looking at each other for a couple of seconds. Maryanne was loth to ask him into the house. She could see no purpose in his visit, other than to disrupt her life, but at the same time politeness dictated that she invite him in. They could not stand looking at each other on the doorstep.

"Won't you come in, please?"

"Er, that could be awkward if your husband is present."

"He is away on duty."

"All right then, if I may."

Maryanne led him into the parlor, and closed the door.

Thomas looked at the chair he was offered, a little longer than was required, before seating himself. He was not used to sitting on such old furniture.

Maryanne offered him a drink, but he declined.

He got straight to business. "Maryanne, since you did not answer my letter, I decided to come and talk to you, to try and bring you round."

Maryanne interrupted. "Thomas, I fear that you trip will have been in vain. I understand that the lifestyle as your wife would have been much more opulent than this" - she waved her hand to take in the house - "but it is the life I have chosen, for better or worse. Unfortunately I met the man on the train before I met you, and he swept me off my feet. If I had met you before him, no doubt the opposite would have happened." She did not believe for a minute what she was saying, but she felt that, in the interests of sparing his feelings as much as possible, she could be allowed a little fabrication. She was convinced that Peter had saved her from a marriage that promised very little in the way of passion or romance. Having now met Thomas in the flesh, she saw no reason to revise that conviction.

"Maryanne, life as the wife of a soldier will not suit you in the long run, I am willing to wager. Not only the tenuous nature of his job, but the low salary, and his frequent absences, will wear you down until you wish you had made another choice."

"Thomas, there is another factor of which you are unaware. I am with child." She moved her hand over her stomach, which was now showing some signs of distension, but which, unless attention were drawn to it and its size explained, could have been assumed to be the result of good living.

Thomas digested this new information. "That does put a slightly different complexion on things, but does not change my overall position. You could give up the child for adoption. In fact, it makes you an even better prospect, from my point of view, since, as mentioned in my first letter to you, I am in need of an heir, and you have now proved yourself capable." He didn't seem to consider the possibility that he himself might not be capable in that area.

The idea of giving up her baby for adoption appalled Maryanne. How could this man assume that the life inside her was just another factor to be removed from the equation? "I would never give up my baby. He or she was conceived out of love, not by accident, and will benefit from the best that I am able to give him. Or her."

"But that is the problem, Maryanne. What will you be able to offer him or her? I know what the salaries are in the local barracks are, and once you have the added expense of one or more children, you will have to take a step down even from this." And he waved his hand to take in the house.

Maryanne realized that she was not getting through to him. He was now exasperating her, and she saw that plain talk was required. "Mr. Worthington, I am afraid that you are under the impression that everything can be reduced to a monetary level. I realize that times will be tough, and I am prepared for that. However, my husband and I have love for, and devotion to each other. May I compare that with the letters you wrote to me. There was no mention of love, passion, commitment, or any of the other things that a woman needs. And even when you come here, to try and talk me around, still you make no mention of anything of the heart. It is all an accounting exercise to you. And the fact that I am pregnant, which is the culmination of what a woman wants from life, is merely an inconvenience to you, and is to be discarded at the earliest opportunity. And, if anything, is proof of my fecundity, and my ability to allow you to pass on your profits to an heir. Thomas, you mentioned in your most recent letter that you had no understanding of women. I am afraid that I must tell you that the situation is worse than you imagined. You have no idea at all of how women work, or what they want. You will need to improve immeasurably in that area before any woman shows any interest in you. Sorry to speak bluntly, but I see that simple protestations on my part are not getting through to you."

Thomas sat there, a little stunned at this tirade. He was not sure how to handle it. Finally he said "I do realize that I am largely inexperienced in affairs of the heart. That is due to a secluded upbringing, and devoting my attentions to my business to the exclusion of all else for the last fifteen years or so. I had hoped that, once we were together, you would show me how these things work, and instruct me in the needs and wants of a woman."

At this, Maryanne felt rather abashed at what she had said. Thomas was finally displaying a human, vulnerable side, and showing that it was not all an accounting exercise to him. She decided to ameliorate her tone. "I'm sure you will find a woman who will be all that you require, and who will lead you through the maze that is a woman's needs and desires. I might have been that woman once, but I am no longer, I am sorry to say."

Thomas saw that there was no point in pursuing this, and he took his leave, rather morosely.

Maryanne sat there for a long time after he had gone. For all his lack of appreciation of her feelings, she felt sorry for him, and she found herself wishing that he found someone who would be the woman he needed.

Chapter 3

As the baby grew inside her, she experienced the usual effects that pregnancy does. She got tired more quickly, with the extra weight she was carrying, and had occasional severe bouts of back pain.

Peter was supportive during this time, even if he could not really understand how it was happening.

They found a midwife living nearby, and made arrangements for her to assist them when the time came.

Finally the day arrived when Maryanne knew that the birth was imminent. Luckily Peter was not on duty, and he was dispatched to summon the midwife.

Maryanne had a relatively easy, but certainly not painless labor, and gave birth to a healthy baby boy. Peter assisted where he was able.

Afterwards, Maryanne lay with the baby on her chest, and looked tenderly at him. "Isn't he beautiful?"

"Yes, I suppose so." Peter found it as difficult to dissemble as Maryanne. He could appreciate that the creation of life was a wonderful and mysterious thing, and was something that only women understood. And that the baby now lying on her had potential to become all sorts of things. But he was not able to consider him beautiful. But Maryanne thought he was, so that was sufficient.

"I've been thinking about names, in case it was a boy. What about 'Albert'? It was my uncle's name."

Once again, Peter didn't have strong feelings on the subject. Albert was as good as Frederick was as good as Joseph. "Yes, that is fine by me."

Maryanne and Peter were about to discover another disadvantage of living far away from family. Maryanne had no mother or similar female assistant to help her in the early days with Albert. She had found a couple of books on the subject of child rearing, and had devoured them, but there is no substitute for experience, and she found herself often at a loss as to what to do in certain situations. She didn't know what most mothers work out with their second or successive children: that babies are a lot more resilient than they seem, and there are not many situations or occurrences that are really serious. Maryanne didn't know this, and she worried every time Albert cried or seemed out of sorts. He thrived, however, and she gradually came to understand what interventions were necessary in which situations.

Peter, however, felt a different dynamic in the house. He began to feel more and more that he was the least important member of the household, and that he was no longer first in Maryanne's affections. She looked at Albert with the same loving tenderness that she used to use with Peter. Now, when she looked at Peter it was a neutral look, or even one of exasperation or irritation when he didn't seem to understand Albert's needs or wants, when Peter occasionally held him or rocked or walked with him. Peter was discovering what every new father discovers: that, at the most basic or animal level, his role of helping to produce the offspring was now complete, and his remaining role was simply to provide, while the female performed the raising of the children. He could see that something like this was happening, but he couldn't understand why the addition of another small member of the family should alter everything so completely. He was fighting millennia of evolution.

And so, since Maryanne seemed to have so little time for him, he began to spend more time at the barracks than previously. He found excuses to stay longer on the days he had to go there, and even occasionally found excuses to go there when he wasn't required at all. The other fathers in the barracks recognized what was going on, but as was the custom in those days, and still is in many ways, they didn't talk about it.

Albert grew steadily, and began to take notice of what was happening around him. As he grew, he seemed to understand that he needed to make an effort to bond with his father, and he would smile and gurgle whenever he saw Peter. This had the effect of slowly bringing Peter around to realizing that Albert was not simply an addition to the family, but was a fully-fledged member and was earning his place. Peter then began to understand Albert better, and respond to his moods and requirements more easily. He spent more time with Albert, and began to find this time more and more rewarding.

One aspect of having children that Maryanne had been warned about, certainly came to pass, and that was the expense of raising children. As it was, Peter's salary had been just enough to keep the two of them. Albert and his occasional unusual needs stretched their budget past breaking, and they had to economize even further. Maryanne reflected that she had been warned about this by more than one person. She, however, felt that it was worth the deprivation. The feeling of being a mother trumped all other considerations.

Chapter 4

One day Albert awoke and didn't seem quite himself. There had been similar days and Maryanne was not particularly concerned. He seemed to improve slightly during the day. The following day, he was definitely not right, and Maryanne became a little worried. On the third day, he was undoubtedly sick, and she took him to see the doctor.

The doctor examined him, and then pronounced that Albert had measles. "There isn't much specific that you can do for him. Keep him quiet and try and feed him. There's every chance that he will recover after about a week."

Both Maryanne and Peter had had measles when they were children, and they had not had complications, so they were not overly worried. On the following day the typical measles rash developed on Albert. When he was not sleeping he seemed to find his unusual-looking skin interesting, and held his arm close to his eyes to inspect it.

Things went like this for a further two days, and then on the following day, Albert showed signs of labored breathing. Maryanne was worried at this, and returned to the doctor.

"Unfortunately, Albert has developed pneumonia, which is a common complication from measles. He needs to be admitted to hospital."

Maryanne replied "We don't have the money to put him in the hospital. Can we not nurse him at home ourselves? My husband is not currently away on duty, so he will be able to help."

"You can, but the nursing staff have more experience in handling this sort of thing. If you really can't afford it, then I'll give you the required medication and you'll have to nurse him yourself."

Maryanne returned with the medication the doctor had prescribed. She told Peter about the situation. "We're going to have to nurse him. And I think we are going to have to watch him continuously. We shall have to take shifts."

She and Peter worked out a routine where each sat next to Albert's crib for a time, while the other slept, or cooked, or relaxed. As much as one can relax when one's child is ill.

Unfortunately, Albert didn't improve. His breathing became more forced. He seemed to be fighting the infection almost physically. He would be restless, and make little violent movements as if he were trying to push the sickness away. Maryanne and Peter watched him, and felt helpless.

During that night Peter was watching him, and noticed that he seemed to be resting better. He seemed to be no longer fighting the infection, and although his breathing was still forced, he seemed to be past the worst. Peter returned to the book he was reading. After about 10 minutes, he looked at Albert, and Albert's chest was not moving at all. Peter jumped up, and picked the child out of his crib. There were no signs of life. "Maryanne, wake up!" he shouted.

Maryanne jumped out of bed. She felt for a pulse. There was none. Albert had gone.

She sank onto the bed and wailed. Peter replaced the lifeless child back in the crib, and sat next to Maryanne. He had no idea what to do. He didn't want to cry, he didn't want to comfort Maryanne. He felt lifeless too. He eventually left the house and walked around the streets, his mind as blank as if he had never had a thought in his life. He moved mechanically, but eventually found himself back at the house. Maryanne was still on the bed, now sobbing quietly. He lay next to her, and put his arm around her. She moved up against him and carried on crying. They lay like that for the rest of the night.

In the morning Peter got up before Maryanne, wrapped Albert's body in a blanket, and took it outside. As soon as the General Store was open, he went and bought some rough wood, and made a rudimentary coffin for Albert. He placed the body in it and nailed it shut. The finality of this act finally broke his defenses, and he sat down and wept.

After a time he went back into the house. Maryanne was awake, but just lying on the bed, looking at the wall.

Later that morning Peter arranged for a funeral, with the same pastor who had married them. While there, Peter spoke to him about Maryanne. "Is there anything I can do to make things easier for her?"

The pastor was sympathetic, but realistic. "You must understand that Maryanne has effectively lost a part of herself. In the same way that Eve was created out of part of Adam, a child is created from part of its mother. She will never get over this completely. The best you can do is to simply be there. She may act oddly, and do things that make no sense to you. Just be sympathetic, and don't try and rush her. She will eventually get nearly back to how she was."

What Peter didn't ask the pastor, was how he was meant to recover from Albert's death himself. As a man he felt that he was meant to keep the ship of his family afloat, without being rocked by the waves. But he had bonded strongly with Albert, after his initial indifference, and he now felt the death keenly. But men were meant to act like men, and so he refrained from mentioning his own state of mind.

Albert's funeral was held three days later. Some of Peter's comrades from his barracks attended, and the landlady that Maryanne had befriended when she first arrived in Omaha. Peter and Maryanne went through with it mechanically, responding to sympathy wishers appropriately, but without even being aware a lot of the time what was happening. Afterwards they returned home, and Maryanne broke down and wept again. Peter wished that he could too, but he felt that he had to be strong. He sat there, feeling helpless.

Chapter 5

The months following Albert's death were quiet, bleak, and grey. Peter and Maryanne hardly spoke to each other, and almost lived separately.

Over the times that Peter was away on duty with the Pacific Railroad, Maryanne sat and looked out the window. She had lost interest in most things, and barely ate enough to keep alive. When Peter was home, they went about their lives, but without enjoyment.

Slowly, however, Maryanne resumed her interest in sewing, and crocheting. She started to make a blanket for them for the upcoming winter months. She started to cook again. While she was certainly not the joyful person she had been, she was definitely on the road to recovery.

Peter however, seemed to be unable to recover. He was moody, and incommunicative, and hardly ever initiated a conversation with Maryanne. He responded to her overtures monosyllabically, and seemed to be unwilling to talk about anything.

One evening Maryanne decided to try and get through to him. She sat next to him. "Peter, dear, you seem to be very morose. Are you still grieving for Albert?"

Peter looked away. He was in a turmoil. Should he break down in front of his wife, and thus display apparent weakness, or should he brazen it out and pretend that he was not unduly affected by Albert's death? Unfortunately he chose the latter path. "It's nothing really. I'm more concerned for you. Are you getting over it?"

If Peter had taken the path he perceived to be the weaker one, the story of Maryanne and Peter's lives would have had a completely different ending. However, for all sorts of reasons - his upbringing, his military training, and others, he decided that he could not confess his innermost feelings to Maryanne, and so the grief carried on festering inside of him.

Maryanne could tell that he was not being fully open with her, but she didn't know how to get him to open up. Their lives carried on as before.

About a month later Peter joined a patrol that went out onto the plains some distance from Omaha, to confront some Indians that were raiding nearby white settlements. He left early in the morning, said a perfunctory goodbye to Maryanne, and was gone. He said that he would most probably be away for about three days.

Maryanne spent that day washing, preserving some fruit, and reading. The next day she was sitting sewing, and around midday, there was a knock at the door. She opened it, and Stephen, one of Peter's comrades, stood there. She took one look at his face, and her legs turned to water.

"Hello, Maryanne, may I come in please?"

"Cer.., certainly." she stammered. She managed to get to a chair herself before slumping into it. She tried not to look at Stephen.

Stephen sat down. "Maryanne, I need to tell you something. I am afraid I am the bearer of bad news." He paused.

Maryanne could feel her throat constricting and her vision blurring. She was close to fainting.

"I am deeply sorry to have to tell you that Peter was shot and killed while we were engaging some Indians, early this morning."

Maryanne caught a sob in her throat. Stephen wondered whether he should comfort her, but felt it would not really be appropriate. He wasn't quite sure what to do. He had never had to perform this kind of duty before.

"I am really sorry. He was a good friend of mine too."

After a minute or two, he felt that there was no point in staying. He stood up. "His funeral will be held at the barracks. I shall come again in the next few days to give you the details." He let himself out.

Maryanne succumbed to a sort of grey semi-consciousness. She wasn't fully awake, but she wasn't asleep either. Her brain slowed down, mercifully sparing her from having to think about anything. She remained in this state of limbo for a couple of hours.

Finally she had to rouse herself. She took to her bed, and fell asleep, and slept the rest of the day, and all night.

The next day she opened her eyes, and remembered everything. She lay there wondering about life. Was there a God, who intentionally gave happiness, in order that he may snatch it away again? Or was it part of some bigger plan, that was meant to prepare one for some future existence? Was there a plan at all? Was there a God at all? She had no answers. All that she knew was that six months ago her life had been idyllic. Now it was shattered.

She dragged herself through that day, and the next one.

On the following day Stephen came to give her details of the funeral, which would be held the following day.

The next day she dressed mechanically, in black. Luckily she had something in black and didn't have to go out and buy a dress. She left the house and walked slowly to the barracks. Stephen met her and guided her to where the funeral was to be held.

She managed to get through the service without breaking down. Afterwards, some of Peter's other brothers-in-arms came and offered their condolences to Maryanne. After most of them had left, she said to Stephen "Did the Indians trap Peter somewhere? How did he actually get shot? I always thought that he was wily enough to avoid getting into a dangerous situation."

"Strange you should ask that! I wasn't sure if I should tell you this or not. But since you asked: the circumstances in which Peter was shot were not typical at all. He was in cover, and would have been perfectly safe if he had stayed there. But for some reason, I'll never know why, he left cover and walked out into an area that was very exposed. And he would have known that. Within seconds he had been spotted by an Indian and they fired. He was down with one bullet. It was almost as if he had wanted to be shot."

Maryanne understood immediately, but didn't say anything to Stephen. If only Peter had opened up to her, and begun the healing over Albert's death. But he decided to do the 'manly' thing and bottle it up. And it festered and grew inside him, until the only way out he could see was to die, as honorably as possible. The news left her desolate. She walked slowly back to the house, hardly noticing the people around her.

Chapter 6

The day after the funeral, Maryanne awoke and lay there pondering on the way her life had changed over the past two years.

From the calm and security of her aunt's house, she had moved to a far more tenuous existence, while being happier than she had ever been. That had now been replaced by grief and loss, while her existence remained tenuous. Where, only just over a year ago, she had wondered whether life could get any better, she now wondered whether life could be any worse. She had lost a child, lost a husband, and had no source of income. The small payout she had received from the army would cover her rent and food for six months at the most, if she lived frugally. But what then? Should she return to stay with her aunt? Or, she tried not to even form the thought in her mind, should she ask Thomas to finally take her as his wife?

She realized that asking Thomas to take her certainly was an option, and one of the better ones available to her. But there were so many reasons that she fought with the idea. Her original reason for rejecting him now seemed relatively trivial. His seeming inability to show love and passion was now hardly worth worrying about. She had had love and passion in abundance, and where had it finally got her? She had loved a child and lost. She had loved a husband and lost. She wondered whether it really would have been better to never have loved at all.

The main reasons she could not countenance throwing herself on Thomas's mercy was the indignity of effectively begging him, now that the roles were reversed, and the real possibility, in fact the better than even chance, that he would refuse or even ignore her request.

However, as the days wore on she slowly came round to the idea. She realized that she would be prostrating herself, but not very much worse than Thomas had prostrated himself to her when he visited her in Omaha. Plus, it was purely between the two of them. It was not as if she was publicizing her request. Whatever his answer, it would be private to them, and she would not have to suffer the judgment or feigned sympathy of other people. Finally, for all his dourness and seeming coldness, he had acted with honor throughout, and she had no reason to imagine that he

would act any differently in this situation.

Finally, she realized that she had nothing to lose. If he refused, she would return to Baltimore.

She sat down and wrote.

Dear Thomas,

It is with great difficulty that I write this letter, as I am sure you will understand once you have read it.

My circumstances are greatly altered since the time you came to see me in Omaha. Since then, I gave birth to a baby boy. At about six months old, however, he became ill, and we could not afford the medical expenses to treat him effectively. He died shortly thereafter. That effectively drove a wedge between my husband and me. Whether it was my own sadness at losing my child, or whether it was his own sadness at the loss, I am not sure, but my husband became withdrawn and incommunicative. Not long after that he was shot and killed while on patrol on the plains. From information gathered from another member of his barracks, it would seem that he could have kept himself out of harm's way, but instead exposed himself to gunfire.

I am thus, circumstantially anyway, back to how I was as I boarded the train in Baltimore. However, I am vastly different in experience. I have loved and lost, and I am ready to seek contentment. I do not desire romance any more. However, I should like to have more children.

And so I come to the main purpose of this letter.

I am writing to say to you that, should you still be in need of a wife, and still feel that I may fill the role, I shall be happy to join you in San Francisco. I do not have the requirements that I mentioned when you visited me here, any longer. However I have learned much about housekeeping and child rearing, and thus should be able to fulfill your requirements, as mentioned in your letters, and on your visit.

Kindly reply soonest, since I shall only have enough money for the train fare should I leave within the next two months. Should I not hear from you within that time, I shall return to Baltimore.

Yours etc.

She re-read what she had written. She felt it struck exactly the right tone. It was not contrite, since she had nothing to be contrite about. It was not supplicatory either. It simply stated the facts, and offered to resume their arrangement, albeit two years later.

She posted it, and carried on with her depressing existence.

Chapter 7

Three weeks later, a letter arrived from San Francisco. Maryanne sat down, too a deep breath, and opened it.

Dear Maryanne,

I am sorry to hear of your recent losses. I cannot imagine what it must be like to lose a child.

I was more than a little surprised to read your offer, since you seemed so adamant that I was not the right man for you when I visited you in Omaha. However, as you point out, circumstances change, and the experiences one has, temper one's needs and wants.

I am still not married. After what you said to me in Omaha I understood that I needed to learn more about the ways of women. However, I could not really see my way clear to doing that easily. I don't mind telling you that I have thought of you often since our meeting in Omaha.

After due consideration, I am willing to accept your offer, and for us to resume our arrangement once you arrive here. Kindly notify me of your arrival date.

Yours etc.

Maryanne sat and read it again. Short and sweet, but all that was necessary, she thought. And he had been thinking of her since his visit! Maybe a heart did beat in that accountant's breast after all!

Maryanne went outside and looked at the sky, or as much as was visible between the buildings. It was a deep blue, and seemed to radiate hope. For the first time in many months she felt that life might improve.

She took a large part of her meager savings, and bought a ticket to San Francisco. However, this time she had to make do with sharing with other women. Needs must. She arranged to terminate the lease on the house, and to sell most of the furniture that she and Peter had bought. She made ready to depart.

She also wrote to her aunt. After informing her of her recent losses, she continued:

After much agonizing, I decided to contact Mr. Worthington again, to see whether he was still in need of a wife, and if so, whether he was interested in our resuming our previous arrangement. He replied in the affirmative, and I am shortly to be leaving Omaha for San Francisco. I have often thought how similar your earlier life and mine are turning out to be. It is as if my sojourn in Omaha provided the experience of love and passion that I needed to have, and allowed me to have my fill. Now, older and wiser, I shall be content with a good, solid man, and hopefully more children. I don't like to think of Omaha simply as a detour on the bigger road of my life, but that is what it seems to have turned out to be.

I shall write again once settled with Thomas.

Yours, etc.

The day of departure arrived. While getting dressed, she remembered that the dress she was wearing was the same one she had on when Peter led her up on to the roof of a rail car, when it had gone through a tunnel and she had got soot everywhere. She smiled ruefully. That all seemed so long ago now. She had lived almost a lifetime since then.

She got a cart to the station, and had her trunk placed in the baggage car. She climbed aboard and joined two other women in a compartment, larger than the one she had been in on her earlier journey.

As the train slowly pulled out of Omaha station, she felt that she was leaving behind a large chunk of her life. Much good, but much bad too. Much like life in general. But it was a sunny day, and she looked to the west and the start of a new chapter.

As they pulled into San Francisco, she saw Thomas waiting on the platform. He had flowers in his hands again. At least he gets that part right, she thought wryly.

She alighted and went up to him.

"Hello Thomas. I am glad to see you again."

"Hello Maryanne, I am glad that you have finally arrived in San Francisco." He bent and kissed her lightly on the cheek, and then proffered the flowers. She took them and smelt them. They had a fresh, clean fragrance.

"Thank you."

Thomas had brought two servants with him, and he instructed them to get Maryanne's trunk. He led her out of the station to a waiting buggy, and helped her aboard.

They rode through the streets and she took in the city. It was much bigger than Omaha, from what she could tell, and it was a lot busier too. At one point in the ride she looked down on the sea, and she realized that she had not seen the sea for two years. Finally they turned into the driveway of one of the larger houses that she had seen. They stopped at the door, and it was opened by a man who looked like a butler.

"Good afternoon, madam!" he said.

"This is James. This is Miss Marston." said Thomas. Then he looked quickly at Maryanne. "Ah, but you're no longer Miss Marston, are you?" he said quietly.

"No, I am not. But it will suffice for now!" she smiled.

Thomas showed her into a hallway, and she met another woman servant, Mabel, who was the housekeeper. Thomas led her up a large staircase, and at the top they turned right. "The main rooms are on that side, and you will have rooms here, for now." He showed her her quarters, each room of which was about the same size as the entire house she had lived in, in Omaha.

"I have arranged a reception for tomorrow night, for you to meet some of my friends and business associates. I hope that that is all right."

"That is fine. I look forward to meeting them. Will, er, the Thackerays be there?"

"Yes, they have indicated their attendance. I think possibly George will take a while to be won over, but Martha is always understanding. I need to now return to the factory, to attend to some business. Please make yourself at home, and ask James or Mabel should you need anything. Actually, that doesn't need to be said, does it? You don't need to make yourself at home, since this is your home!" He gave Maryanne a quick hug, and then left.

Maryanne sat on the bed and looked about her. The difference from her room in Omaha was marked. Apart from the size, everything about it was obviously good quality. The furniture, the bedding, the carpet, all were of a high standard.

She lay back on the bed and wondered whether she actually deserved all this. And she resolved then to make Thomas a good wife, and to contribute to his life, and life in San Francisco generally, as much as she was able.

Chapter 8

Arrangements for the wedding began almost immediately. Thomas had chosen a local church for the ceremony, but took Maryanne there to check whether she approved of it. She did.

He took her to a dress shop and left her there to be measured for her wedding dress. He then fetched her and they went to discuss food with the caterers. Then, on the way home, they went to visit his mother.

Maryanne had had no experience of mothers-in-law. Peter's parents were both dead by the time she met him. She knew that mothers- and daughters-in-law often did not get on well, and she realized that the circumstances of her marriage to Thomas would not count in her favor, but she resolved to do her utmost to befriend Thomas's mother and bring her round.

They stopped the buggy at a pleasant looking house. Not as big as Thomas's, but undoubtedly well-appointed. Thomas led the way to the door, and knocked. An elderly, well preserved lady, about 70 years old, answered.

"Hello mother!"

"Hello Thomas. Let me unlock the door." She rattled a key in the lock, and opened it.

"Mother, I should like to introduce my fiancé, Maryanne. Maryanne, my mother."

"How do you do, Mrs. Worthington?" said Maryanne, proffering her hand. Mrs. Worthington took it briefly.

"Do come in." She led the way into a small but tastefully furnished parlor. "Let me set the tea things."

While Mrs. Worthington busied herself in the kitchen, Maryanne looked around. She saw a young boy in a picture on the mantelpiece. "Is that you?"

"Yes, that's me, fishing in the Patapsco. I never actually told you, did I, that we came from Baltimore originally. That's one of the reasons that your profile on Brides-by-Mail caught my eye."

"Indeed! And there I was, thinking it was my natural beauty!"

Thomas laughed heartily. "It was that that distinguished you from all the other girls from Baltimore!"

Mrs. Worthington sat down and started pouring the tea. "So tell me, my dear, I believe you've had a checkered journey from Baltimore to San Francisco."

Nothing like getting straight to the point, thought Maryanne. She looked quickly at Thomas. She wasn't sure whether her mother-in-law knew her entire past. Thomas's face was inscrutable. Oh well, she thought, no point in avoiding it, best to talk about it now.

"I have indeed. I don't know of anyone else who took two years to do it!" She related the basic story of her sojourn in Omaha, while playing down the fact that she had been on her way to meet Thomas when it began. Thomas could tell her about that, if necessary.

"So you lost your little boy! That is so tragic. I can empathize, since we lost Thomas's twin brother at a similar age. Also pneumonia from measles, as it happens. They both contracted measles, but only little James got pneumonia. That's one of the reasons that Thomas has had a rather sheltered and protected upbringing. We didn't want to lose him too."

"Do you find that you ever got over it?" enquired Maryanne.

"No, my dear, you never fully get over it. I still dream about James occasionally. One gets on with life, but the memory remains. Luckily Thomas has succeeded enough for two sons, so that makes it a little easier." She patted Thomas's knee, and he smiled, having heard this many times before.

"It was devastating losing little Albert, but it showed me one thing at least. I enjoy being a mother. I found it rewarding and interesting. So I hope to be able to provide Thomas with a few heirs at least, and some grandchildren for you."

"Thank you my dear, that will make me very happy."

From her initial coolness, Mrs. Worthington had thawed towards Maryanne on the strength of their shared tragedy. Maryanne understood that her mother-in-law was on her side, and she was grateful for that.

The reception that Thomas mentioned was held that night. About twenty couples, friends and associates of Thomas's, had been invited.

Maryanne shook hands and smiled at them all. She had checked before with Thomas as to how much she should talk about the past two years. He said that it was not necessary to go into any details, but to just tell them that she had been living in Omaha for the duration.

Obviously, however, one couple knew the whole story. When she greeted George and Martha Thackeray she wasn't sure what she was going to say.

"Hello George. Hello Martha. Wonderful to see you again." She thought that that sounded rather lame.

"Hello," said George rather stiffly.

"Hello Maryanne." said Martha. "So sorry to hear of your recent losses."

"Thank you."

After she had greeted the rest of the gathering, Martha came up to her, and steered her away to one side. "I can see such a change in Thomas already! He has cheered up considerably since the last time we saw him."

"I am glad of that. Tell me, how did he take it when you broke the news to him at the end of your train journey from Baltimore?"

"He looked crestfallen. He was standing there with a bunch of flowers in his hand. He saw us, and we walked towards him. He was still looking up and down the train for you as we reached him. When we told him you weren't there he was nonplussed. He could not understand what it was that could change your mind. I tried to explain, but he doesn't really understand women! Hopefully you will now be able to teach him something!"

"Did he tell you that he came to see me in Omaha?"

"No, really? Did he? No, he never mentioned that."

"Yes, about four months afterwards. I was pregnant. He tried to get me to change my mind, without understanding the reasons for my action. I eventually had to spell it out for him. I felt a bit of a heel. But I think I finally got through to him."

"Yes, he understands business issues immediately, but when it comes to people he has to have things explained more than once!"

"And the rest of the time these past two years? Did he never speak about finding someone else?"

"No, actually. And he mentioned you a few times. I think he hoped that you would still finally change your mind. Obviously he never wished the tragedies on you that did happen. But it seems that his patience has finally been rewarded, not so?"

"I suppose so. And George? He seems not to have forgiven me."

"Oh, don't worry about George. He understands women even less than Thomas! He'll thaw over time."

They returned to join the rest of the party.

Maryanne surveyed the group that would be her friends from now on. There were one or two couples that seemed to be close to her age, and she made a point of engaging them in conversation. She would obviously have a duty, as Thomas's wife, to be friendly to his friends, and be the charming hostess, but by the end of the evening she felt that there were definitely some people there that she could relate to. They were not the kind of people who would have lived in a tiny clapboard house on a side street, as she and Peter did in Omaha. But they were the kind of people that her aunt and her might have known back in Baltimore. She was already feeling at home.

Chapter 9

A month after Maryanne's arrival in San Francisco, the wedding took place.

Maryanne wore a pink wedding dress, in keeping with her status as having been married before, and walked down the aisle alone. She had asked Martha to be her Matron of Honor.

The house was gaily decorated for the reception, and there was food and drink in abundance. There were about a hundred guests, and many of them remarked upon how happy and contented Thomas looked, especially compared with the last couple of years.

The bridal couple left for their honeymoon the following day, taking the train south to Los Angeles. They stayed there for three weeks, going to the theatre, art galleries, and restaurants. Thomas also asked, very apologetically, if Maryanne would mind if he visited a few potential customers for his factory. She even accompanied him on one of these trips.

They returned to San Francisco refreshed.

Maryanne settled into life with Thomas. He would go to his factory every day during the week. She stayed at home and busied herself with sewing, reading, and she also decided to learn to play the piano. She engaged a tutor to teach her weekly, and she spent a lot of time practicing.

In the evenings they would have dinner together, and then read, or she would play the piece she had been practicing, for him.

On weekends they would visit friends, or have friends to visit, attend the occasional concert or play, and go for walks in one of the parks, or along the beach promenade.

Maryanne found herself slowly warming to Thomas. Initially she had looked upon this marriage as one almost of necessity; as being required to save her from penury or having to return to live with her aunt. But as the months wore on, her prior indifference to Thomas became affection, and finally love. She understood that it was not the same love that she had had for Peter in the early days of their marriage. That had been a heady, breathless sort of love. But she now knew that that sort of love never remained for long. It couldn't, by definition, since it relied on novelty, and being with someone that one was still getting to know. Once one knew that person well, and there was nothing novel left to do, the headiness had to come down to a regular, day to day sort of togetherness. With relationships that began that way, there was always a vague feeling of disappointment, in that one was aware of its inexorable reduction in intensity, and one wished that it could somehow remain at the initial level.

However, with the sort of relationship she had with Thomas, it improved with time, and thus one was aware of almost a gratitude, that life could improve, rather than deteriorate.

About six months after the wedding, she awoke one day feeling a bit different. This time she knew what it almost certainly was. She waited a few more days, and when it did not change, she went to check with the doctor. He confirmed her suspicions.

That evening, at dinner, Maryanne decided to tease Thomas. "Thomas, dear, do you think this dining table is big enough?"

"Er, big enough for what, my dear?"

"For the extra person who will be joining us soon!"

Thomas looked a little mystified, and then realization dawned. "Really! Are you with child? That is wonderful!" He got up and went and hugged Maryanne around the shoulders. Later that evening they sat on the couch together and discussed how the baby's room should be decorated, and what the child would be named, depending on its gender.

Maryanne had an uneventful pregnancy, and an uncomplicated birth. She produced a boy, which made Thomas very happy. They called him Julian.

At about six months, he also contracted measles, but this time he was whisked off to hospital at the first sign, and recovered without any lasting ill effects.

With the experience from her first child, Maryanne found raising Julian a lot easier, and with help from the servants, she had a relatively easy time as a mother.

Chapter 10

When Julian was about three, Maryanne decided that the time had come to make a trip back to Baltimore to visit her aunt. She corresponded with her, and arrangements were made. Thomas saw the two of them off at the station, and they settled in to the journey. They had a compartment to themselves. Julian was fascinated by everything connected with the train ride, and Maryanne found vicarious pleasure in his interest. He was full of questions, which she answered as best she could.

On the afternoon of the second day the train stopped in Omaha, and since it was going to be there for about an hour, Maryanne and Julian left the train and walked into the town. Not a lot had changed since she was last there. After looking at a few of the shops, they headed for the cemetery. Maryanne had not intended to make any such pilgrimage, but now that she was here, she wanted to go. She found the two graves - Peter's one, and Albert's tiny one.

"Why is this one so small?" asked Julian.

"Because he was only a baby when he died." she explained. She read the birth and death dates on the headstone to Julian.

"I thought babies could never die!"

If only, thought Maryanne. She hugged Julian close, and was thankful for him.

Back on the train, she decided to make a memory for Julian. She took him to the coupling between their car and the adjacent one. She then put him on the ladder going up to the roof, and they slowly made their way up it together, with her behind Julian to protect him. They carried on until their heads emerged above the roof and the wind tousled their hair. Julian loved it, and Maryanne's hair swirled around his face. Maryanne remembered when she did this with Peter, and how they had gone into a tunnel as well, and emerged with soot everywhere.

The sun was about to set just then, and she and Julian watched as the light turned from bright to orange, to gold. She thought about her time with Peter and Albert, and about Omaha. It was as if, while watching the sun, she was finally setting to rest that time, and was letting it go. It was a very freeing thing.

Just after the sun actually set, she and Julian climbed back down again.

Two days later they arrived in Baltimore, and hired a buggy to take them to her aunt's house. Maryanne knocked at the door.

Aunt Hilda opened it. She had aged quite a lot since Maryanne last saw her. "Hello, Aunt! Good to see you after so long! This is Julian. Julian, say hello to your Great-Aunt Hilda."

"Hello." said Julian shyly. Then he turned to Maryanne. "Why is she great? What has she done?"

"She raised me! That's what!" said Maryanne, laughing.

They went into the parlor and sat down. Julian went to explore the garden at the back of the house.

"So, my dear, you have had a whole life's experience since you left. I am sorry for the tragedy you have gone through, but it would seem to me that everything has finally turned out for the best. Am I right?"

"You are indeed. And it is very much as you said it would be. The love and passion that Peter and I had was overpowering in a way, but it satisfied my hunger for such a relationship. Now, with Thomas, life is much more stable, predictable, and easier. I do not hanker for novelty. It's not as if life is boring. Far from it. There is much to do each day that is new. But the affinity between Thomas and me is constant, well-founded, and reliable. I do love him, in a different way, but just as much, as I loved Peter."

"I am so glad that you have finally arrived at a happy place, my dear."

"The only question that remains for me now, is this: when I have a daughter, how do I explain this to her, to save her from having to go through the same tragedy that I did?"

"You can't, my dear. I tried it with you. It didn't work. You have to allow your children to make their own mistakes!"

Maryanne nodded. She finally understood that to be true.

www.ingramcontent.com/pod-product-compliance
Lightning Source LLC
LaVergne TN
LVHW041632070526
838199LV00052B/3320